THE THIRD TURTLEDOVE

Story & Illustrations
by Danie Connolly

Absolutely Perfect Publishing
139 Summer Street, Kennebunk, ME 04043
www.danieconnolly.com

ISBN number 978-0-9970546-2-0

Designed by Aikman Design

Summary:
Armed with her suitcases, fluffy pink slippers and her favorite plant, Momma Turtledove seeks a quiet corner of the Peartree after the holidays only to find it's more chaotic than she could ever image! This frolicking tale of the Twelve Days of Christmas takes a hilarious trip up and down every branch of this Holiday Christmas Tree!

"How you do with what you have is who you are."

Much love to my grandkiddos from GranDanie.
Always be kind and you'll always be happy.

To BBB, Thanks for being the string
to my balloon . . . Sweet Dan

It was the second day of Christmas and the two Turtledoves were snuggling while taking a nap on a comfortable branch in the Peartree.

They were worn out by the hustle and bustle of the holidays. Just then there was a fluttering sound of wings and the patter of little feet.

"I thought I'd never get here!" a tiny voice chirped.

"Momma Turtledove!" they tweeted in complete surprise. "What are you doing here? You're not due to arrive for another two weeks!"

"I couldn't stay at your brother's Peartree another second. I'm exhausted from the gift wrapping, decorating, cooking dinners, washing clothes and babysitting," she replied.

"It was all I could do to slip away when I did," she added. "All I want is a little peace and quiet."

"You're just in time for the Peartree Ball. You'll have to join us! There's a very nice neighbor upstairs," they chirped excitedly. "He's the..."

"NO THANK YOU!" she interrupted. "The last thing I need is a date. I just want to rest my weary feathers on a nice little branch."

"We'll be at the party at the top of the Peartree," said the two Turtledoves.

She gathered up her suitcases, favorite pillow, pink slippers and a potted plant she never traveled without, hopped down and waddled over to a little branch near the center of the tree.

After she carefully tucked in her belongings, she fluffed her favorite pillow, closed her eyes and began to peacefully drift off to sleep.

Suddenly there was a sound of loud clucking. Momma Turtledove sat up to see what the commotion was about. Three fashionably dressed French Hens were perched on the branch above, carrying dozens of hat boxes and garment bags.

"Bonjour! Bonjour! Bonjour! We are the Three French Hens!" they cackled. "We just arrived from Paris and are so excited about zee dance tonight. Come see what we bought. Fabulous, oui?"

"I'm sure they're darling dresses, but I'm a little tired and I want to sleep in my..."

"You must come to zee dance tonight. Perhaps something new and wonderful to wear will change your mind?" They held a brightly colored dress up to her.

"No thank you. All I want to wear is my pillow."

"But we are going dancing with the Four Calling Birds and there are only three of us. Please? Please? Please?" The sound of flittering wings made them scurry to the end of the branches.

"Hello... Hello... Hello... Hello... any of you chicks in there?" The Four Calling Birds had arrived.

They looked comical with telephones cords wrapped around them everywhere.

They cawed and cackled and cracked jokes the entire time as they tried to straighten themselves out.

Momma Turtledove did her best to untangle them. When she was finished she plopped down on a nearby branch.

"Hey, Momma Turtledove," they chirped, "why don't you put your dancing shoes on and party with us?"

"All I want to wear are my fluffy pink slippers." She gently guided them out and waved them away. "You go and have a nice time. I'll clean up this mess."

Momma Turtledove looked around at the chaos. There were boxes and ribbons everywhere. She sighed and began folding the tissue paper. As she was stacking the hat boxes, she heard a bell ring.

She hopped down to a lower branch and discovered a huge box tied with a bright red ribbon. A sign on top read OPEN IMMEDIATELY!

Quickly she untied the ribbon and discovered Five Gold Rings. "Oh my, this is too much for me to handle alone." Unfortunately, everyone had left.

Somehow she found the energy to hang the Five Gold Rings on the branches.

The little Turtledove could barely lift her wings by the time she finished. Slowly she made her way back to her corner of the tree and began to snooze.

"Hello...anybody home? We need help!" Momma Turtledove sprang to her feet. She couldn't believe her eyes. Six Geese Laying stood before her!

"We're about to lay our eggs! Do you have any spare nests around? We're in a hurry."

"Oh my, oh my," she fretted. Then she remembered the hatboxes the Three French Hens had brought from Paris. "Wait here and I'll be right back!" And off she flew.

Minutes later the Geese delivered six of the biggest eggs she had ever seen.

"We should be tired but we feel marvelous," the Six Geese Laying said.

"Would you mind if we slipped out to the Peartree Ball to catch up with the rest of our feathered friends?"

"Why would I mind? It's not like I'm on a vacation or anything," she muttered.

The tired little Turtledove dragged herself back to her perch. Droplets of water fell on her face and she dreamt it was raining.

Opening one eye, she gazed up to find Seven Swans Swimming staring at her.

"Are you the maid?" they asked. "We just swam up the coast for the dance and need you to wash these towels."

Momma Turtledove looked at them in sheer disbelief.

"And make sure they're nice and fluffy!" they reminded her as they sashayed out.

The little Turtledove shrugged her shoulders and dragged the towels to the washing machine. One hour later, the towels were nice and warm and fluffy.

She stacked the towels on top of each other but they kept tipping over.

Momma Turtledove had a great idea. She tiptoed over to the hat boxes and placed a warm towel over each egg.

There was even an extra towel for her to curl up under for a long nap.

Finally, it was nice and peaceful. She could rest.

Suddenly she heard a strange noise. It sounded like moooooooo. She rubbed her eyes. It sounded like there were cows in the Peartree!

"Oh no, oh no...this is not a good place for milking!" she said, scaring Eight Maids Milking away.

The sleepy little Turtledove looked up and saw eight cows and milk pails standing on the Peartree's branches.

Just as she was about to call the Eight Maids Milking back to get their cows, Nine Ladies Dancing entered.

They kicked up their heels and knocked over the pails of milk. It splashed everywhere.

"Look at the mess you're making!" Momma Turtledove threw her towel on a branch and started mopping up the milk.

The Nine Ladies Dancing were gaily bounding about the Peartree in their dancing shoes. They were slipping and sliding and laughing.

Splish! Splash! Splish! Splash! Splish! Splash! Splish! Splash! Splish!

Momma Turtledove shooed them away, and headed back to her branch.

"Finally," she sighed to her potted plant. "Now I'll get some peace and quiet!"

Out of nowhere, Ten Lords Leaping appeared to the sound of far-off music and began leaping from one branch to another.

She was worried about the Ten Lords Leaping knocking the sleeping eggs out of their hat boxes.

"Out! Everybody out!" squawked Momma Turtledove, flapping her wings.

As Momma Turtledove was ushering them out, she was met by Eleven Pipers Piping marching straight towards her.

"About face," she commanded.

They turned around and marched back out, but not before knocking a few Gold Rings off the tree.

She scurried up the branches and rehung them. She was exhausted but slowly crawled back to her pillow.

Nothing could wake her up now.

Nothing — except for what happened next...

Twelve Drummers Drumming were leading a parade throughout the Peartree!

The little Turtledove spied everyone marching behind them, including Eleven Pipers Piping, Ten Lords Leaping, Nine Ladies Dancing, Eight Maids Milking, Seven Swans Swimming, Six Geese Laying, Five Gold Rings shaking, Four Calling Birds, Three French Hens and the Two Turtledoves!

The tree began shaking violently. Momma Turtledove was knocked off her perch and onto the sidewalk.

A second later, her suitcases, favorite pillow and potted plant plopped down next to her!

In a daze, Momma Turtledove gathered her belongings and rushed to the curb.

"Taxi!" she cried. A big yellow taxi came to a screeching halt. She jumped inside and told the driver to take her to the airport... pronto!

"Visiting with the family?" the driver asked as he pulled away from the curb.

Momma Turtledove blurted out the entire story. "...and to make matters worse, they wanted to fix me up with some birdbrain who lived upstairs."

She settled back on the seat and stared at the taxicab driver's ID. His name was A. Partridge. "Any chance you live in the crazy Peartree?" she gasped.

"Not during the holidays!" He chuckled, "I stay clear of there!"

They arrived at the airport terminal, and the driver turned to ask, "So, see you next year?"

Momma Turtledove gathered up her belongings and chirped, "You bet, I wouldn't miss it for the world!"

THE END!

Danie Connolly always enjoys the exuberance of little kids! She's spent over 40 years writing and illustrating children's storybooks, hoping to make them smile and giggle even more! She is an award-winning playwright, whose works has been staged for children and adults throughout New England. She has also written humor columns for national magazines and newspapers, and writes articles for boxing magazines.

Connolly has authored and illustrated children's storybooks, taught art to Alzheimer's patients, painted wall murals for hospitals, created theatrical backdrops and props and designed costumes for children's plays. As a photojournalist, she has been recognized for her exhibits; Norman Rockwell's Small Town America – recreating the iconic *Saturday Evening Post* covers with local town characters; Holiday Dos – everything Christmas adorned on heads; and Hollywood Goes to the Dogs – showcasing man's best friends in movie poster recreations.

Absolutely Perfect Publishing creates Tubestories, the line of children's storybooks and greeting cards based on some of the outrageous characters from her books and plays.

Danie Connolly is the proud GranDanie of six very special grandkiddos, and resides on the Southern Maine coast with her husband Bob and three very spoiled Scottish Terriers.

BOOKS BY DANIE CONNOLLY

A Hop, Skip and Jump, Jump, Jump!
Dum Dum Deedlebird
Everybody's Puppy – Nobody's Dog
Happy Birthday to U!
Loser Louis
Now Appearing...The Ants
On the Road to Life
Rainbow Junkyard
Ribbit
Snarls
Teardrop Stew
The Bald Headed Eagle that Refused to be Bald
The Great Soapino
The Case of the Missing Sock
The Day Bradley Lost His Imagination
The Poker Was Framed!
The Silverware

HOLIDAY BOOKS
Heartseeds
The Littlest Christmas Tree
Miss L. Toes
Recycled Angels
The Reindeer Hop
Reindeer Sniffles
S.A.N.T.A.
The Great Christmas Cookie Escape
The Snowmen of Kindness
The Stained Glass Angel
The 13th Day of Christmas
The Third Turtle Dove
Twinkles
Red Lights
Thomas T. Turkey